NOTE TO PARENTS

Learning to read is an important skill for all children. It is a big milestone that you can help your child reach. The Richard Scarry Easy Reader program is designed to support you and your child through this process. Developed by reading specialists, each book in the series includes carefully selected words and sentence structures to help children advance from beginner to intermediate to proficient readers.

Here are some tips to keep in mind as you read these books with your child:

First, preview the book together. Read the title. Then look at the cover. Ask your child, "What is happening on the cover? What do you think this book is about?"

Next, skim through the pages of the book and look at the illustrations. This will help your child use the illustrations to understand the story.

Then encourage your child to read. If he or she stumbles over words, try some of these strategies:

- **Use the pictures as clues**
- **Point out words that are repeated**
- **Sound out difficult words**
- **Break up bigger words into smaller chunks**
- **Use the context to lend meaning**

Finally, find out if your child understands what he or she is reading. After you have finished reading, ask, "What happened in this book?"

Above all, understand that each child learns to read at a different rate. Make sure to praise your young reader and provide encouragement along the way!

Introduce Your Child to Reading
Simple words and simple sentences encourage beginning readers to sound out words.

Your Child Starts to Read
Slightly more difficult words in simple sentences help new readers build confidence.

Your Child Reads with Help
More complex words and sentences and longer text lengths help young readers reach reading proficiency.

RICHARD SCARRY'S
Great Big Schoolhouse
Readers

Get That Hat!

Illustrated by Huck Scarry
Written by Erica Farber

STERLING CHILDREN'S BOOKS
New York

Lowly has a hat.
Lowly likes that hat.

The wind likes that hat, too.
WHOOSH!

The wind blows.
The hat blows away.

Oh, no!
Get that hat!

5

The hat is in a tree.

It is up, up, up.

A bird is in the tree.

It is up, up, up.

Huckle goes up, up, up.

TWEET! TWEET!

The bird flies away.

The hat flies away, too.

Oh, no!

Get that hat!

Huckle and Lowly go, go, go.

Bridget and Arthur go, go, go.

The bird and the hat go, go, go.

The hat falls.

It falls on a car.

The car goes.
Oh, no!
Get that hat!

The car goes fast.

The hat goes fast.

The car stops.

The hat falls!

It falls in the mud.

Huckle and Lowly run.

Bridget and Arthur run.

Too late!

Up goes the mud.

Up goes the hat.

Down goes the mud.

SPLAT!

There goes that hat!

Up go Huckle and Lowly.

Up go Arthur and Bridget.

WHOOSH goes the wind!
There goes that hat!

The hat falls.

It falls on a head.

It is not Lowly's head.

It is Molly's head.

Silly hat!

Lowly puts on the hat.
Lowly likes that hat.

The wind likes that hat, too.

The wind blows.

The hat blows away.

Oh, no! Get that hat!

STERLING CHILDREN'S BOOKS

New York

An Imprint of Sterling Publishing
387 Park Avenue South
New York, NY 10016

ISBN 978-1-4027-9918-1 (hardcover)
ISBN 978-1-4027-9919-8 (paperback)

Produced by

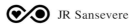 JR Sansevere

Distributed in Canada by Sterling Publishing
C/o Canadian Manda Group, 165 Dufferin Street
Toronto, Ontario, Canada M6K 3H6
Distributed in the United Kingdom by GMC Distribution Services
Castle Place, 166 High Street, Lewes, East Sussex, England BN7 1XU
Distributed in Australia by Capricorn Link (Australia) Pty. Ltd.
P.O. Box 704, Windsor, NSW 2756, Australia

For information about custom editions, special sales, premium and corporate purchases,
please contact Sterling Special Sales at 800-805-5489 or specialsales@sterlingpublishing.com.

Manufactured in China

Lot #:
2 4 6 8 10 9 7 5 3 1
11/14

www.sterlingpublishing.com/kids

RICHARD SCARRY'S
Great Big Schoolhouse
Readers

One of the best-selling children's author/illustrators of all time, Richard Scarry has taught generations of children about the world around them—from the alphabet to counting, identifying colors, and even exploring a day at school.

Though Scarry's books are educational, they are beloved for their charming characters, wacky sense of humor, and frenetic energy. Scarry considered himself an entertainer first, and an educator second. He once said, "Everything has an educational value if you look for it. But it's the FUN I want to get across."

A prolific artist, Richard Scarry created more than 300 books, and they have sold over 200 million copies worldwide and have been translated into 30 languages. Richard Scarry died in 1994, but his incredible legacy continues with new books illustrated by his son, Huck Scarry.